PLAYTIME?

JEFF MACK

Philomel Books

For Wesley

PHILOMEL BOOKS

an imprint of Penguin Random House LLC
375 Hudson Street, New York, NY 10014

Copyright © 2016 by Jeff Mack.

Philomel Books is a registered trademark of Penguin Random House LLC.

Library of Congress Cataloging-in-Publication Data is
available upon request.

Manufactured in China by RR Donnelley Asia Printing
Solutions Ltd.
ISBN 978-0-399-17598-5

10 9 8 7 6 5 4 3 2 1

Edited by Michael Green.
Design by Jeff Mack and Semadar Megged.
The art was created using mixed media, including pencil,
watercolor, collage, and digital manipulations.

BedTime.

Shh...
Bedtime.
Bedtime.